WHOA JEALOUSY!

by
Woodleigh
Marx
Hubbard
with
Madeleine
Houston

G. P. Putnam's Sons   New York

Gratitude to Nancy Paulsen, Cecilia Yung and Andrea Brown.
And a final farewell to Zeb and Lily, two good dogs.

Printed in Hong Kong by South China Printing Co. (1988) Ltd.
Book designed by Gina DiMassi. Text set in Steam.
The art was done in gouache and watercolor pencil on Fabriano paper.
Library of Congress Cataloging-in-Publication Data
Hubbard, Woodleigh. Whoa, jealousy! / by Woodleigh Marx Hubbard;
with Madeleine Houston. p. cm. Summary: Jealousy, envy, greed, and rivalry
come into a person's life in the forms
of various animals and all kinds of bad things happen.
[1. Emotions—Fiction. 2. Behavior—Fiction.]
I. Houston, Madeleine. II. Title. PZ7.H8624 Je 2002 [E]—dc21 00-045906
ISBN 0-399-23435-7
1 3 5 7 9 10 8 6 4 2
First Impression

For Oliver Wink, my Esteemed Pug
Who wags his tail when he sees my mug
—W. M. H.

To the teachers of metaphor.
—M. H.

Jealousy is a feeling that gets inside you.

You hear it at the door.
    You aren't expecting visitors,
        so you ignore it.

But Jealousy is still there.

PECK
    PECK
        PECK

You open the door
                just
                    a
                        crack.

The face of Jealousy
    at first seems kind of sweet.

You invite it in, and suddenly . . .

There's a No~Good Dirty Nasty Mean
Feather~Faced Chicken

filling up your living room!!

But Jealousy is too chicken
to work alone.
This fowl~mouthed critter
gets on the phone.
Bawk Bawk

It calls up all its friends.
Bawk

Bawk

Bawk

And before long . . .

Bawk
Bawk

a whole gang
is in your
kitchen,
   cooking up
    trouble
   and making
    a mess
   of things!

First comes Envy.

Envy is a Sneaky,

Creepy,

Sharp~Tongued Snake.

LOOK OUT!

Envy slips in through
the floorboards
and slithers up your skin
and hisses into your ear.

Suzanne is cooler

Daniel is quicker

Stephanie is smarter

Sallie is taller

Envy crowns you
King of Mean and Queen of Misery.

But this King and Queen
have nothing
and feel worthless.

So when Greed comes to visit,
the door is already open.

Greed is a **Rude Rat**.
It pokes its nose in your face,
twitching its whiskers.

Greed wants more.
You give it a little something
and it wants more.
You give it more and
it
wants
MORE.

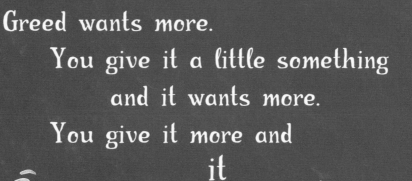

gimme
gimme
gimme

me ME ME

ALL MINE

Greed doesn't say "Please,"

it says, *Please ME!*
Make ME happy!

Before long, you're spending all your time
trying to keep Greed happy.
You forget about your family,
your friends, your pets, your sports,
because Greed demands

ALL
your attention.

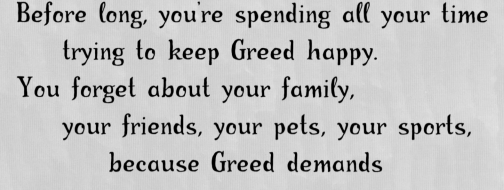

But Greed is never happy,
because it can
NEVER get enough.

And that's when Rivalry arrives.

Rivalry is an **Angry Red Hornet**.
It buzzes through the window
and hums around your head.

It razzes you and frazzles you over what

they've

done and said.

Rivalry has a NASTY sting.

Rivalry is **MAD** at happy people,
so it backbites and lies.
It wants to be the **ONLY** winner,
so it doesn't play fair.

It hurts people that get in its way,
so all your friends leave.

And now . . .

here you are.

All by yourself,
except for . . .

a MEAN CHICKEN
a SNEAKY SNAKE
a RUDE RAT
and a
MAD HORNET!!

How

MISERABLE!

Even

your

DOG

doesn't

want

to

be

around!

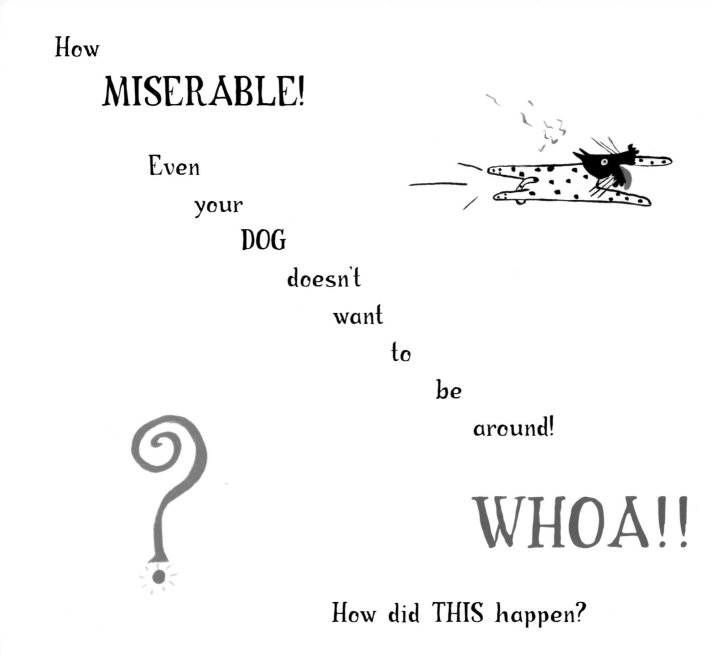

?

WHOA!!

How did THIS happen?

Well . . .
if you look back . . .
you'll see that
YOU let them in.

But listen: YOU have a choice.
You let them in . . .
and YOU can

KICK

THEM

OUT!

But wait:

Sooner or later,

Jealousy, Envy, Greed and Rivalry come back.

You know what can happen. So before they get in . . .

Pluck **that** Chicken!

Knot **that** Snake!

Trap that Rat
in a very small space!

And **swat** that Hornet
right out of this place!

Hooray! you say.

"I'm STRONG today!

I got rid of those bullies!
I'm free to play!"

But
be
careful!